The Story of Black Beauty

Illustrated by Alan Marks

Based on the story
by Anna Sewell

As a young horse, I was gloriously happy.
I played with other colts by day
and slept by my mother's side at night.

Then, one day, a man
came to our farm.
"Beautiful!" he said,
stroking the white
star on my forehead.
"I'll buy him."

"Be brave, Black Beauty," said my mother.
"All young horses must leave their mothers,
and make their way in the world."

"Just remember – never bite, or rear, or kick.
And, whatever happens, always do your best."

I was taken to a grand house, many miles away.

"He can pull my carriage, along with Ginger,"
declared my new owner, Lady Richmore.
"Put him in a bearing rein, so his head is held high."

The groom, Reuben, pulled my head back
and fixed the rein – tight. I felt red-hot pain.

"I'm sorry, Black Beauty," said Ginger.
"You haven't come to a good home."

Every day we went out in the carriage.
With our heads held back,
    it was hard for us to take the strain.

As the strength drained out of us,
Reuben would whip us on.

"Can't you be kinder to the horses?"
begged Joe, the young groom.

"QUIET!" snarled Reuben.
"What do you know about horses?"

Joe was the only kind person in that house.

Whenever he could,
he would slip away
and feed us juicy
apples and carrots.

But the day came when Ginger
couldn't bear it any longer.

With a wild neigh, she reared up.
Our carriage toppled over
and broke to pieces.

Ginger was taken away forever.

After that, Joe left as well. I was all alone.

Reuben paid me no attention,
    so he didn't notice when my shoe became loose...

Late one night, I stumbled on some sharp stones.
Reuben was thrown to the ground.

"Another useless horse!" snapped Lady Richmore, the next day.

"I'll sell him to the first fool who wants him.
He won't get a grand home now, of course...
not with a bad temper and ruined knees."

I was put in a horse sale.

A kind-looking man paid a few coins
for me and took me away.

His name was Jerry
and he lived in London.
"I want you to be my
cab horse," he said.

We worked hard,
out all day in all weather.

But I didn't mind,
because Jerry and
his family were so
good to me.

Once, I saw an old, worn-out chestnut. Its eyes had a dull, hopeless look. Then I heard a whisper,

"Black Beauty... Is that you?"

It was Ginger! She told me she belonged to a cruel driver who whipped her and overworked her.

"You used to stand up for yourself," I said.

"I did once, but now I'm just tired," she replied.

"No, Ginger!" I cried. "You must keep going.
Better times will come."

"I hope they do for you, Black Beauty,"
she whispered.

"Goodbye and good luck."

One day, a customer asked Jerry
to be the groom at her house
in the country.

He couldn't take me – she already had a horse.
"Sorry," Jerry comforted me.
"I hope someone kind will buy you."

But my new master was a cruel man.
If I was too slow, he whipped me, hard.
In the end, I simply collapsed in the street.

As I lay there,
barely breathing,
a cool hand stroked my neck.

It was a horse doctor.
He helped me to my feet
and took me to his stables.

"I'm going to make you better,"
he told me. "I know just
the home for you."

My new owners
were two sisters.
"What a dear
face he has,"
they cried.

Their groom led
me to the stable and
began to brush me.
Soon, he came to
the white star
on my forehead.

"Black Beauty! Is that you? Do you remember me? It's young Joe...
I can't believe I've found you after all this time."

I've been here for a year now. Joe is always gentle, the sisters are kind and my work is easy.

Best of all, they've promised never to sell me.

I've found my home at last.

Anna Sewell lived from 1820-1874.
She adored horses and hated the cruel way
they were treated. She wrote "Black Beauty"
to make people more caring about horses.
The book was a huge success and changed
the way people thought about animals.

Taken from an adaptation by Mary Sebag-Montefiore

Edited by Jenny Tyler and Susanna Davidson

Designed by Emily Bornoff

This edition first published in 2012 by Usborne Publishing Ltd, 83-85 Saffron Hill, London EC1N 8RT, England.
www.usborne.com Copyright © 2012, 2008 Usborne Publishing Ltd. The name Usborne and the devices 🎈 👍 are Trade Marks
of Usborne Publishing Ltd. All rights reserved. No part of this publication may be reproduced, stored in a retrieval
system, or transmitted in any form or by any means, electronic, mechanical, photocopying, recording or otherwise,
without the prior permission of the publisher. First published in America in 2012. UE.